W9-CFC-467

DRAGONBREATH
CURSE OF THE
WERE-WIENER

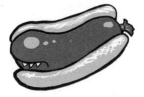

Sturges

DRAGONBREATH
CURSE OF THE WERE-WIENER

BY
URSULA VERNON

SCHOLASTIC INC.

For Kevin, who cooked while I painted

No part of this publication may be reproduced, stored
in a retrieval system, or transmitted in any form or by any
means, electronic, mechanical, photocopying, recording,
or otherwise, without written permission of the publisher.
For information regarding permission, write to Dial Books
for Young Readers, a division of Penguin Young Readers
Group, a member of Penguin Group (USA) Inc.,
345 Hudson Street, New York, NY 10014.

ISBN 978-0-545-29951-0

Copyright © 2010 by Ursula Vernon. All rights reserved.
Published by Scholastic Inc., 557 Broadway, New York,
NY 10012, by arrangement with Dial Books for Young
Readers, a division of Penguin Young Readers Group,
a member of Penguin Group (USA) Inc. SCHOLASTIC
and associated logos are trademarks and/or registered
trademarks of Scholastic Inc.

12 11 10 9 8 7 6 5 4 3 2 1   13 14 15 16 17 18/0

Printed in the U.S.A.   40

First Scholastic paperback printing, January 2013

Designed by Jennifer Kelly
Text set in Stempel Schneidler

DARING DANNY DRAGONBREATH HIKED
THROUGH THE DARK AND CREEPY WOODS.

THERE WAS SOMETHING WRONG WITH THE TREES, BUT DANNY DIDN'T KNOW WHAT IT WAS.

THERE WAS SOMETHING WRONG WITH WENDELL TOO.

PREMONITION (WHATEVER THAT IS)

"What is your problem?" asked Danny's best friend, Wendell, shaking him awake.

Danny Dragonbreath woke with a start.

"Huhzz? What?" He blinked at the iguana. "Wendell?"

"You fell asleep on the bus," said Wendell, leaning back. "And then you started flailing and saying my name, and you're just lucky I woke you up before anybody heard. Sheesh. How embarrassing."

Danny rubbed the back of his neck and then put his hand over his stomach. He'd been having some kind of nightmare—something about the moon and Wendell.

And he remembered spooky woods. Not the fun Halloween kind of spooky, but the *real* kind of spooky, dark and dripping wet.

He couldn't remember what had been happening in the woods, but it was bad, whatever it was.

Danny looked out the window. It was a gray day, but it hadn't rained yet. Of course Wendell had brought his umbrella with him anyway. Wendell's umbrella—which his mother had picked out—had a map of the world on it. (Wendell's house also had shower curtains with a map of the solar system on them, and periodic-table place mats. That was just the sort of person Wendell's mother was.)

"Well?" said Wendell, poking him with the umbrella.

"I had a really weird nightmare," said Danny.

Wendell waited.

"You were in it. We were in a dark forest, and something was wrong."

Wendell waited.

After a minute, the iguana said, "That's it? That's all?"

"What?" asked Danny defensively. "It was totally scary!"

He had to admit that once he'd said it out loud, it didn't sound nearly scary enough.

Wendell put his hands on his hips. "It was scary. That's it? No elaborate stories of monsters and quicksand and lightning and having to cross rivers of hot lava by jumping on the heads of ravenous lava earwigs the size of cows, with pincers made out of giant steel knives?"

"Well, no . . ." said Danny, "but that would be pretty cool. Especially the lava earwigs! I never knew you had it in you, Wendell! What do lava earwigs eat, you think?"

"People," said Wendell. "No, wait, it'd be too hard to eat people all the time if you lived in hot lava. They'd have to survive on some kind of rocks, I suppose."

"But they'd eat people when they could get them," said Danny, waving his hands. "Like ice cream! I bet if you lived in lava and ate hot rocks all day, people would taste cool and refreshing. Different people would be different flavors too. Spicy Dragon . . . Vanilla Iguana . . . Chocolate Chip Salamander . . ."

The bus arrived at school, cutting short more speculation on the life and times of the Giant Lava Earwig, but Danny was feeling better anyway. Lava earwigs were much more interesting than vague dreams about woods and Wendell.

There was still a nagging uneasiness buried at the bottom of his mind, like the old papers at the bottom of his locker. But it was easy enough to ignore. Danny had heard of the word "premonition" but thought it had something to do with car engines. Wendell *did* know what the word meant, but he didn't believe in premonitions.

A STRANGE HOT DOG

The line for lunch was nearly to the door, which was normal, and the hot dogs were large and bright red, which was not normal. Danny poked his lunch a few times and thought he felt it twitch.

"There's something weird about the hot dogs," he said to Wendell.

"Weird how?" asked Wendell, who brought his lunch. His bologna sandwich was cut into neat triangles, again, courtesy of his mother. Danny would bet money that there was a neatly folded napkin in Wendell's lunch box, possibly with a map of the solar system on it.

"Take a look. Doesn't the color strike you as sort of . . . unnatural?"

"It's a hot dog," said Wendell, but peered over at Danny's lunch anyway. "Oh. Hmm." He shoved his glasses up on his nose and picked up the hot dog warily. "You're right. That's not normal hot dog color." He handed it back to Danny.

"Looks sort of like . . . blood," said Danny.

"Anyway," Wendell said, "it looks more like a candy-apple red to me—OW!"

"What? What?"

Wendell jerked his hand away from the hot dog and shoved a finger into his mouth. "Owwwmmmff!" he said around the mouthful of finger.

"Are you okay?"

I THINK IT BIT ME!

Danny considered this. On the one hand, hot dogs didn't usually bite. On the other hand, Wendell was not what their teacher Mr. Snaug called "a fantasy-prone personality." (Mr. Snaug did call Danny this on a regular basis, generally in notes sent home to Danny's parents.)

Besides, it wouldn't be the first time the school lunch had fought back. There had been that incident last spring.

"You remember the potato salad?"

"The one that bit Big Eddy?" Wendell nodded.

"Yeah. I thought it escaped into the storm drain, though."

"It did. And anyway, everybody knows that potato salad and hot dogs are mortal enemies," said Danny.

"You're lucky I'm in too much pain to ask how you know that."

"Let me see your hand."

Danny peered over the wound. Sure enough, there was a semicircular row of little red dents, with a tiny bead of blood at the bottom of each one. "Holy cow, I think it did bite you."

"Should I go to the nurse?" asked Wendell worriedly. "What if I catch some horrible hot-dog-borne illness?"

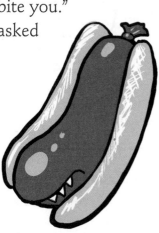

"Wiener pox," said Danny gravely, tapping his snout. "Kills thousands every year. The government hushes it up."

"I think I have some bandages in my locker..."
Wendell glanced suspiciously at the now-quiet
hot dog. "Are you gonna eat that?"

"After it bit you?" Danny considered. "I dunno.
Feels sort of like . . . long-distance cannibalism."
He held it up in one hand.

"What are you—"

"Wait for it . . ."

Big Eddy the Komodo dragon, the school bully, stalked by a minute later and plucked the hot dog out of Danny's hand. "Thanks, dorkbreath," he sneered.

"Oh, no. You have taken my lunch. Stop," recited Danny in a monotone.

Big Eddy looked briefly confused, but settled for slapping Danny on the back of the head and stomping off.

DO YOU EVER WORRY THAT YOUR CHILDHOOD IS WARPING YOU IN SOME FASHION?

ARE YOU KIDDING? I'M COUNTING ON IT.

Wendell did indeed have bandages in his locker—three boxes worth. Danny peered over the iguana's shoulder with mild awe.

"Are those periodic-table bandages?"

"Mom buys them," said Wendell, sighing. He slapped the atomic weight of chromium on his wound.

"Your mom has issues."

"You have no idea . . ."

THE MORPHING

Danny woke up the next day feeling a little off. Not bad, exactly, not unsettled the way he had been the previous morning on the bus, just . . . off.

He went down to breakfast and found his mother snoring into her coffee. Danny's dad was away on a business trip, and Danny's mother did not do mornings well.

Toast. Toast seemed like a good idea. He slid some bread into the toaster.

"Zzz . . . zz . . ."

It was taking forever for the toast to pop up.
Danny rubbed the back of his neck. Something
just wasn't quite right. His mom sat at the end of
the table with her claws around a cup of coffee,
looking like death only partially warmed over.

"Are you . . ." He stopped. He wasn't sure what he wanted to ask. "Is everything okay?"

Something in his voice must have alerted her. She opened an eye and made an effort to focus on him. "M'fine. Morning. Y'know." She dipped her tongue into her coffee.

Danny wished his dad were home and cooking breakfast—bacon and eggs might go a long way toward chasing the last bits of his nightmare away. He could talk to his mom about it, and she'd probably make an effort to wake up and listen, but he didn't know what he'd say. *I had a night-mare and it was scary but I don't really remember why* seemed sort of vague, not to mention babyish.

After a minor eternity, the toast popped up. Danny buttered it thoughtfully. Had he had another nightmare? He didn't remember dreaming at all.

"Are you okay?" his mother asked, making a Herculean effort to wake up.

Danny nodded, then shrugged. "Yeah. Just...I dunno. You know, some mornings you just don't feel right."

"That's every morning," muttered Mrs. Dragon-breath, sinking lower into her chair with her coffee.

Normally Danny would have enjoyed the walk to the bus stop, but it was a gray, gray day, and it left him in a gray, gray mood that his usual cheerfulness couldn't shake. The sky couldn't decide if

it was raining or not.
Occasional raindrops
splattered on his head
and on the pavement,
but not quite enough to
justify getting out an
umbrella.

It was drizzling, he
decided. He felt like he was drizzling too. (His
head, not his body—that would have just been
disgusting.)

After about ten minutes, the drizzle increased
to something close to plain old rain. Danny gave
up toughing it out and dug around in his backpack for his umbrella.

One side of it was sort of broken from the time
he and Wendell had an umbrella fight, but it kept
the rain off.

Wendell was already at the bus stop, slumped
against the sign. He looked even more miserable
than usual, which for Wendell was saying some-

thing. Most iguanas had a sort of gloomy look anyway, but Wendell seemed to feel that if he was miserable in advance, life would go easier on him.

He didn't even look up when Danny approached.

"Wendell? Buddy?"

Danny waved a hand in front of the iguana's face. "Wendell?"

"Oh. Hey." Wendell twisted the straps of his backpack between his hands. "It's you."

Danny didn't exactly expect a wild greeting in the morning—Wendell dancing around and cheering would have been weird—but this was worrisome. "Are you okay?"

"I . . . I have a problem," said Wendell.

Danny opened his mouth to say that Wendell had a lot of problems, most of them mental, but the expression on the iguana's face stopped him. "Really?"

Wendell looked around nervously. There was no one else at the bus stop, but he still lowered his voice.

"Promise you won't tell anybody?"

"Dragon's honor."

Wendell sighed, turned around, and pulled his shirt up.

"Wendell!" Danny put a hand up to his mouth involuntarily.

"Keep your voice down!" hissed Wendell, yanking his shirt quickly back down.

"No! We're reptiles, same as everybody!" Wendell crossed his arms, looking defiant and miserable all at once. "And look at my hot dog bite!"

Danny leaned forward. "Oh man..."

The wound was puffy and looked a little swollen, like a mosquito bite. But more importantly, the entire thing was bright red. Not infected red, but an unnatural, candy-apple red...a very familiar shade...

"Wendell! Dude! That's the same color as the hot dog!"

"I know!" said Wendell.

"Did you tell your mom?"

"Yeah. She called the doctor and they said some redness was normal for an insect bite. She didn't see the hot dog, so she thinks it was a bug." Wendell tucked his hand into his armpit.

"Does it hurt?"

"No. Kinda itches, though."

"There's something very weird going on here," said Danny, not without some delight. "And we're going to get to the bottom of it!"

"I want to go to the hospital," said Wendell.

The dragon put his hands on his hips. "And say what? They're never going to believe it was a hot dog bite."

LUNCH LADIES

"This is a terrible plan," said Wendell.

"It's a great plan," said Danny. "Where's your sense of adventure?"

"I think you killed it that time you said we should build a catapult."

"It was a great catapult."

Wendell realized that he was on the losing side of history regarding the Avocado Catapult Incident, and went back to his original complaint. "Besides, you never said how we were going to get into the lunchroom and get a look at those hot dogs. They don't let kids back there. Ms. Woggenthal will throw you out on your tail." (Ms. Woggenthal was a matronly salamander who always wore a hairnet, despite not having any hair. She ran the lunchroom with an iron fist and plastic gloves.)

"That," said Danny with relish, "is the cleverest and sneakiest part of my plan."

Wendell heaved a sigh and waited, like a kid seeing a tetanus shot in his not-too-distant future. "Yes?"

"You're on the yearbook committee."

Wendell folded his arms. "I don't like where this is going."

"Oh, come on. You go to the lunchroom. You turn on the charm. You tell Ms. Woggenthal that you're doing a special section on lunch, and that you want some photos of the lovely ladies of the lunchroom."

Wendell wavered.

Danny played his last card. "Do you really want to shave your back for the rest of your life?"

Danny lurked behind the door while the iguana talked to Ms. Woggenthal. He had to admit, when Wendell put his mind to something, he really gave it his all.

"So," Wendell finished up, "we were thinking of a little spotlight on the people who feed us lunch every day. The school chefs! The people who make it all happen!" He held up his fingers at right angles, looking through the little window as if it were a camera. "I was hoping I could get some ideas for shots back in the kitchen, and then we'll come back next week when we've got the section approved and take a few photos."

Danny rolled his eyes. If he'd tried this, he'd have been thrown out so fast, his tail would smoke. But of course, because it was Wendell—

"That sounds nice," said Ms. Woggenthal, patting girlishly at her hairnet. "Come on back."

Wendell winked at Danny behind the door and followed the lady salamander into the kitchen, leaving the door open behind him. "Thank you, Ms. Woggenthal. Would you mind answering a few questions as well? For instance, how do you come up with these masterpieces? The cheese wrap last week was exquisite!"

Their voices receded. Danny waited a moment, then poked his head around the door.

Wendell had Ms. Woggenthal on the other side of the room. "Stand right there," he said, again holding up his fingers. "I'm seeing a photo with you at the table here, perhaps with a ladle in one hand, or a spatula—"

Danny slipped through the door and hurried

across the room. There was a short corridor, and the big walk-in freezer stood at the end of it, cold and silver . . . and shut tight.

"Well," Danny muttered under his breath, "nothing ventured, nothing gained..." It was one of his mother's favorite sayings. Whenever she said it, his father would reply with "Fools rush in," but Danny didn't think that was terribly productive under the circumstances.

He pulled the freezer open as quietly as possible, wincing at the squeak of the handle and the pop of the door's rubber lining. He opened the door just wide enough to squeeze through, then pulled it shut behind him.

The light went out.

Danny made a noise that he was very glad Wendell wasn't around to hear. Not that he was scared or anything. It was just . . . unexpected. Startling. And cold. Yep, it must have been the cold that made him squeak like that.

He rummaged around for the wall and a light switch. Icy metal shelves met his hands, and bags of plastic covered with frost.

It was incredibly cold.

At last his fingers found the light switch, and he snapped it on. He was surrounded by tightly packed metal shelves covered with boxes and bags. His breath steamed out in clouds as he read the labels on the boxes, looking for hot dogs. He hoped they weren't in the back. His dragonish metabolism generally kept him pretty warm—he hardly ever needed a sweater in the winter—but it was really cold in the freezer. Plus a lunch lady might come in at any minute. He sighed, a little smoke mixing in with the steam.

When he finally found the boxes, Danny could have kicked himself—of course they were right on the floor in front of him—they'd been serving hot dogs yesterday, after all.

"GRADE B WIENERS—400 COUNT" the box proclaimed in bold letters.

This wasn't terribly helpful. Danny walked around the stack and crouched down to read the back of one of the boxes. Maybe there'd be something there—ingredients, warnings, something he could take back to Wendell.

But the back of the box was blank. Danny chewed on his lower lip. Maybe there was another box somewhere—

The freezer door opened.

"I don't know, Mabel," said the lunch lady over her shoulder, stepping into the freezer, "I thought there was another bag in here." She turned back and grumbled. "Somebody always forgets to turn the light off."

Danny huddled into the smallest ball he could manage behind the stack of boxes, not daring to breathe, lest the steam give him away.

"Coleslaw . . . " she muttered, scanning the shelves, "coleslaw, coleslaw, where's the coleslaw . . . I don't want to dig through the Big Freezer . . . "

Please hurry, Danny pleaded silently, feeling his chest tighten as he held his breath.

"Aha!"

She grabbed a bag off the shelf. It squished unpleasantly when she hoisted it. Danny hadn't realized that coleslaw came in bags. There was something nasty about a whole bag of slaw squelching.

The lunch lady opened the door, and without glancing in Danny's direction, flicked the light off and left.

Danny exhaled, feeling light-headed.

He tried to feel his way back to the light switch but tripped over a pile of boxes. Card-

board crunched, and something cold and hard rolled under his foot. It felt pretty much exactly the way a frozen hot dog would. Danny winced.

He made it to the light switch.

The boxes were scattered around the floor. The box he'd stepped in had broken open, and a pack of hot dogs had fallen out.

He picked up the package. It didn't say "GRADE B WIENERS." It said something quite different.

LUNCH MEATS

"Were-wieners," said Wendell thoughtfully, turning the package over in his hands.

"Dude, I was afraid they were going to catch me. I barely got out of there." Danny felt that Wendell was skipping over his heroism a little too quickly.

FROM TRANSYLVANIA.

"Were-wieners . . ." muttered Wendell again, scratching at the hair on his back. "Does this mean I'm going to turn into a were-hot-dog?"

"That would be wicked!"

Wendell stared at him.

"Just picture it! The full moon! The light streams down through the window. The iguana sits in his room, looking normal. All is right with the world. And then! Suddenly! Without warning!" Danny flailed his arms. Other students in the hallway glanced over at the wildly flailing dragon, saw that it was Danny, and looked away again.

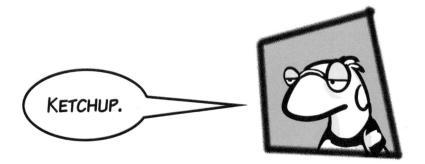

KETCHUP.

"Oh. Hm." Danny considered. "I guess it's not quite like being a werewolf, is it? No legs, for one thing . . ."

"That's what we have to find out," said Wendell grimly, shoving his glasses up on his nose.

FORTUNATELY, I HAVE A PLAN.

LYCAN-SOMETHING

"The library?" Danny could hardly contain his dismay. "You're making us stay after school to go to the library?"

"All knowledge is contained in the card catalog." Wendell went to an open computer terminal and began typing.

Danny loitered behind him and wondered if he could sneak over to the science fiction section before Wendell noticed.

He'd gotten several feet and was just about to begin strolling away when Wendell scrawled something on a scrap of paper, stood up, and collared him.

"Come on. It's in Mythology and Folklore."

Danny cheered up a bit. Mythology and Folklore was probably the most fun of the nonfiction section, after the books about dinosaurs and wild animals. He followed the iguana between the shelves.

"Werewolves . . . werewolves . . ." Wendell ran his finger along a shelf. "Here we go." He pulled down three books and handed one to Danny.

Danny stared at his book, which was titled *A Child's Garden of Lycanthropy.* "What's lycanthropy?"

"Werewolfism."

"Neat!"

"Flip through it and see if there's anything about were-wieners," Wendell ordered, sitting down on the floor.

Danny obeyed.

The book was fascinating. "Did you know that they

have were-leopards in Africa?" Danny said. "Isn't that awesome?"

"Riveting," said Wendell in the tone of one who is not in the least bit riveted. He was working his way through the index of a large book with a plain black cover. What Danny could see of the page was covered in tiny dense print. The dragon shuddered and turned back to the illustrated were-leopards.

"There's nothing in here about were-wieners..." Danny said after a while. "The last entry is for 'were-whales.' But dude! Were-whales! Can you imagine?"

"Seems very inconvenient," said Wendell.

Danny thought about this. "Well . . . yeah . . . you'd need a really big swimming pool..."

WERE-WHALE

ONE OF THE RAREST OF LYCANTHROPES, THE MIGHTY WERE-WHALE HAUNTS THE OCEANS DURING THE FULL MOON. EASILY IDENTIFIED ON LAND BY PERSISTENT KRILL-BREATH, WERE-WHALES CAN ONLY BE SLAIN WITH A SILVER HARPOON.

"Nothing," said Wendell in disgust, slamming the covers of his book shut. "No were-wiener anywhere."

"Could you try curing, y'know, general lycan—ly—werewolfiness?"

Wendell shook his head. "Not without knowing more. It's very specific. You can cure being a werewolf with wolfsbane, but to fix a were-jaguar you have to steal his jaguar-skin cloak—which also works with were-swans. And to cure a bakeneko—a Japanese were-cat—you have to cut its tail off."

"Hmmm. I see the problem." Danny considered. Cutting Wendell's tail off seemed awfully drastic, and Wendell's mother was bound to blame him, no matter how many periodic-table bandages they put on the stump.

"I can't even find anything that might be remotely related to were-wieners. The closest I can find is a legend that you can supposedly get lycanthropy by eating the brain of a wolf."

Danny had a cast-iron stomach, but the notion that he'd routinely been eating wolf brains on a bun since kindergarten did give him a bit of an internal twinge. "Yecck."

"Tell me about it." Wendell gnawed on a clawtip.

"Well!" Danny leaped to his feet. "We're not going to take this lying down. We'll go clear to Transylvania if that's what it takes!"

1-800-HELP

"You mean we don't have a single relative in Transylvania?" Danny couldn't believe it. "Mom! Are you sure?"

Danny's mother gave him a mild look. "Not that I can think of, no."

"Third cousin? Roommate from college? This is important!"

She sighed.

"What about Dad's side of the family? He does have really sharp teeth."

"He's a dragon, Danny."

"I'm afraid I can't think of anything, dear. Now please, I'm trying to get this article finished ..."

Danny plodded downstairs to deliver the bad news to Wendell.

"Apparently we don't have any relatives there. I'm sorry, Wendell, I thought—I mean, we've got them all over, and it's Transylvania, which is crazy with mythical stuff, you'd think we would—"

"Oh." Wendell stared blankly at Danny, and then at the ceiling. After a minute he slid a hand under his shirt and began scratching. "So that's it then. I'm going to become a were-hot-dog."

Danny couldn't take it.

"We'll go to Transylvania anyway," said Danny. "I'm sure the bus goes there. We'll find the—the hot dog farm, or factory, or ranch or wherever they make hot dogs, and we'll make them give us the cure!"

IT MIGHT BE DANGEROUS ...

YOU WANT TO SPEND EVERY FULL MOON BATHING IN MUSTARD?

POINT TAKEN.

Danny pulled out his crumpled bus schedule and went through it. "Transylvania ... Transylvania ... well, crud."

Wendell put his head in his hands, not sure if he should be feeling relief or despair. "There's no bus to Transylvania?"

"Not directly. We'll have to take a transfer. Err . . . two transfers." Danny shoved the bus schedule back into his pocket. "There's one that leaves from the mall, but it'll take a while. Um. Quite a while, actually." He patted Wendell on the shoulder. "Don't worry though, buddy. We'll get you to Transylvania or die trying!"

"Do you know anything about Transylvania?" asked Wendell, staring out the window and contemplating a future that included shaving his back.

THEY HAVE VAMPIRES. DRACULA'S FROM THERE. APPARENTLY THEY MAKE WERE-HOT-DOGS.

"Maybe there's another option," said Wendell, pulling out the package of were-wieners. It was starting to thaw. He shook hot dog juice off his fingers, grimacing. Then he turned the package over. "Look, there's a note here ..."

"A note?"

"Yeah. Under the ingredients. It says 'In case of missing product, damage, or lycanthropy, call 1-800-WURST-R-US.'"

Danny frowned. "You want to call the 1-800-number?"

"Well, it does say 'in case of lycanthropy.'"

"What if they're in on it? What if it's a diabolical plot to enslave the kids of the world through the diabolical arm of the cafeteria?"

Danny heaved a sigh. Calling the company did not hold the same appeal as storming a factory in the vampire-ridden Carpathians. Still, he wasn't the one turning into a were-hot-dog, which was kind of a shame, because he secretly suspected that he'd enjoy it much more than Wendell.

"Fine, we'll use the phone in the kitchen."

Wendell pulled the phone down, checked the number, and dialed. Danny crowded up next to him to listen, but the iguana obstinately retained control of the mouthpiece.

"Wurst-R-Us, Reginald speaking."

"Hello," said Wendell, taking a deep breath. "I'm calling because of the note on the packaging—the one about lycanthropy—"

There was a sigh from the other end. "Another batch? What's the serial number?"

"Um..." Wendell turned the package over until he found the numbers stamped on the end. He read them off to the operator.

There was a rustle on the other end, as if the speaker had turned away from the phone, and they heard, distantly, "Vlad! Another batch of the were-wieners went feral!" followed by even more distant cursing.

"Thank you for informing us," said Reginald, coming back on the phone. "If you cut off the end of the package, you can mail it to us, and we'll send you a full refund, plus a free gift certificate for Wurst-R-Us's new chokewurst, containing artichoke hearts and cheese, perfect for family gatherings, parties, grilling—"

"I don't want a gift certificate!" Wendell broke in. "I want a cure!"

There was a lengthy pause. "Look, kid, it's the gift certificate or nothing," said Reginald, sounding tired. "We don't have the budget to come out and take down your alpha wurst for you."

"The pack leader," said Reginald. "If you kill the alpha wurst, the rest of the hot dogs lose their power."

"Will that cure my lycanthropy?" asked Wendell.

"Yeah, it should." There was another pause, and then Reginald said, "Look, corporate will have my head for telling you this, but you don't have long. The incubation period for lycanthropy is three days. You have to find the alpha wurst before then."

"I don't even know where it is!" said Wendell, frightened.

"They don't like to travel," said Reginald. "Comes of having no legs. It's probably got a den near where the packages were opened."

"The school cafeteria!" said Danny, punching the air.

"Cafeteria?" Reginald sounded worried. "If it was a big batch, then anybody who ate an infected wiener—or was bitten by one—could be changing soon. The alpha wurst can control them. They'll try to protect it."

"It's already been a day and a half . . ." whispered the iguana in horror.

"You don't have long, then," said Reginald.

Danny yanked the phone from Wendell's limp fingers. "Reginald! Danny Dragonbreath here—how do we kill the alpha wurst?"

"Silver skewers," said Reginald. "Holy water mixed with mustard might also work. You won't be able to get close enough, though, not after a day and a half. Not without help. It's probably already got minions."

"Thanks," said Danny.

"Good luck," said Reginald, and hung up.

Danny hung up too and then started plotting.
"Okay, silver skewer, mustard, and holy water."
There was just one thing bothering him.

WENDELL? WHAT'S A MINION?

AN EVIL SERVANT.

...OH.

THE WORST WURST

"A day and a half..." moaned Wendell, slumping back against the counter and putting his face in his hands. "In just a day and a half, I'll be a permanently hairy were-minion under the control of the alpha wurst."

Danny didn't know why Wendell was always so negative. A day and a half was a pretty long time, especially when you were at school. Time always moved extra slowly there. Math class in particular took several centuries a day. He tried to comfort the iguana.

Danny wondered what it said about their friendship, if Wendell was more worried about the goldfish he'd won at the fair years ago than about biting Danny. Still, his best friend was probably just distraught.

"It'll be okay," the dragon said firmly. "We just have to stop the alpha wurst. We need silver."

Wendell considered. "Well . . . there's the silver-ware my grandmother left us . . ."

"Is it real silver?"

The iguana shrugged. "Mom always calls it 'the good silver,' so probably. It's in a box in the china cabinet."

"Good. That's a start."

NOW WE JUST HAVE TO FIGURE OUT WHAT TO DO ABOUT THE MINIONS . . .

"Should we tell the school? Maybe they could stop it . . ."

Danny gave Wendell the withering look this deserved. "Do you think grown-ups can really be trusted with this?"

Wendell sighed.

"No," said Danny, "no, we'll have to enlist the aid of the ancient enemy of the hot dog."

It took Wendell a minute, and then he remembered. "You mean potato salad?"

"The batch last spring. It's in the storm drains somewhere."

"Why would it help us?"

"We let it go!" said Danny indignantly. "Are you implying that it can't feel gratitude, just because it's potato salad?"

"No, but . . ." Wendell spread his hands, wondering how he got into these conversations in the first place. "How do we find it? What if it's dead?"

"Don't be ridiculous," said Danny, heading for the door, "you can't kill a potato salad."

HOW DO YOU *KNOW* THESE THINGS?

"I can see a problem already," said Wendell a few minutes later as he and Danny stood on the curb and looked down into the storm drain.

"Hmm," said Danny, unwilling to admit defeat, but not entirely sure what to do next. "This is the drain where I saw the potato salad . . ."

The opening to the drains was a large rectangle cut in the curb, and it looked big enough for a small dragon or iguana to wiggle into. The problem was the weather. It had been raining all day, and the water was pouring into the storm drain.

"We could go anyway," said Danny dubiously. "I mean, it'll be wet, but I'm game . . ."

Wendell shook his head. "Some of the drains are probably flooded. And if the rain really started coming down, we could drown under there."

"Hmm," said Danny again, more gloomily.

"It's supposed to be sunny tomorrow," offered Wendell.

"Well . . ." said Danny slowly, "I guess . . . if I spend the night at your house tomorrow, we

can sneak out tomorrow night and get the potato salad, and then try to take out the alpha wurst over lunch the next day. But by then it will have been almost exactly three days."

Wendell chewed on his lower lip.

"It's up to you," said Danny.

I'M NOT THE ONE WHO'S GROWING HAIR.

"We don't have any choice," the iguana said finally, scratching at the hair in question. "The important thing is to kill the were-wiener. Even if I've—if I'm a—well, anyway, if you can take down the alpha, Reginald said that would fix it."

"Well," said Danny, "if we go tomorrow night, we'll have time . . ."

83

ITCHING AND SCRATCHING

"You look terrible," Danny said to Wendell at lunch the next day.

"Thanks. I feel terrible." Wendell itched irritably under his shirt.

"Your eyes are all red and you were scratching all through class—"

"Thank you, yes, I was there!" The iguana hunched over his lunch, glaring at his sandwich.

"Looks like you're not the only one," said Danny, glancing around the lunchroom.

Wendell dragged himself from his personal misery to peer across the cafeteria.

It looked like a mass outbreak of lizard pox. Every table had somebody itching furiously. One

of the little skink girls was sitting in a pile of shed scales and looked ready to cry.

"This is bad," said Wendell.

"Yeah, this is worse than the time Christiana Vanderpool got scale lice and infected the whole fourth grade," said Danny, slightly awestruck.

"No," said Wendell, "you don't understand. Look." He pointed at Big Eddy, who had actual tufts of hair sticking out from under his shirt, and was digging at his scalp like he was mining for gold.

"Ha! Big Eddy's growing hair!" whispered Danny.

"That means Big Eddy's going to be a werewiener!" hissed Wendell. "All these kids are going to be were-wieners!"

"Oh no," said Danny. "That means the alpha wurst will be able to control them!"

"They'll all be minions!" Wendell put a hand over his mouth. "*We'll* ... all ... be minions ..."

"But you can't breathe fire!" Wendell said, scratching hopelessly. "Not reliably, anyway."

Danny sighed. Wendell was right. His one spectacular fire-breathing episode had been underwater, at a giant squid. Other than a few really vigorous sneezes, he hadn't managed so much as a spark since. "I can do it if I have to," he said, hoping it was true.

Class had never lasted so long, or seemed so pointless. Danny fidgeted restlessly in his chair. Wendell scratched. Nobody noticed, because half the class was scratching too.

This is useless! Danny wanted to yell as Mr. Snaug droned on about something—the stratosphere or adding fractions or something. *Don't you see the class has lycanthro—lycatrop—lyka—werewolfism!?*

The only thing that kept him from leaping onto his chair and shouting that out loud—other than the fact that he couldn't pronounce the word, even inside his head—was that if he did, he'd probably get after-school detention. And tonight of all nights, he couldn't afford to be late, or have his mom get wind of any trouble. She'd agreed to let him spend the night at Wendell's, but if he came home with notes about yelling gibberish in class, she might reconsider.

He sank lower in his seat and fidgeted.

He tried to settle himself down—Mr. Snaug was giving him that tired look that came before the yelling—by thinking about the supplies they'd need in the sewer. Rope. He had rope, even if it was mostly knots. Flashlight. He had a flashlight. He might need new batteries, but that was fine, there were dozens of remote-controlled toys strewn about the floor of his room. Weapons?

What kind of weapons did you use on a potato salad, anyway?

Danny supposed he could find something in the way of a giant spoon, but his mom would get suspicious if he was rummaging around in the kitchen drawers. She'd stopped believing his claims that whatever he was doing was completely and totally harmless, after the incident with the exploding melon-baller.

Maybe Tabasco sauce would be enough . . .

Besides, the potato salad should remember them. They'd set it free, sort of! Surely it would be grateful.

If it wasn't, they were going to be stuck in the sewer system with an angry salad, and that didn't really bear thinking about.

He chewed on a claw and looked hopefully at the clock.

Less than a minute left.

"Homework for tonight," said Mr. Snaug. "Read the rest of chapter ten, which goes into greater detail about what we've been discussing."

Whatever that was, Danny thought.

"There will be a quiz—"

The bell rang.

"—so don't forget..."

Mr. Snaug probably had more to say, but Danny lunged for the door and was gone.

SLEEPOVER

"Now, you're sure you'll be okay, boys?"

"We're fine, Mom," said Wendell wearily.

"You don't need any more snacks?"

"No, Mom."

"You've both got enough hot cocoa?"

"Yes, Mom."

"And you'll remember to brush your teeth?"

"Yes, Mom."

"All right, then." She planted a kiss on top of Wendell's head, which he bore stoically, and waved to Danny. "Good night, boys!"

Years of nighttime misadventure had taught Danny that Wendell's house was the best place to sneak out of. While Wendell's mom fretted over everything, checked on them every fifteen minutes, and insisted on fluffing Wendell's pillows and checking his sheets,* she also went to sleep by nine, and she slept like a log.

Danny's mother, on the other hand, was good about leaving them alone, but she stayed up until well after midnight and tended to notice the sort of thumping noises that come from—to choose an example completely and totally at random— a small dragon and an iguana climbing out the second-story window, down a tree, and going over the back fence. Living with Danny had really sharpened her hearing.

"How are you feeling?" asked Danny, after Wendell's mom had finally left.

"Itchy," said Wendell. "Other than that, I think I'm okay." Both boys threw on their clothes.

---

* Wendell's sheets had a map of the world, with Antarctica on the pillow

WELL, I *WAS.*

Danny grinned and dug into his backpack. "Bungee cords...check," he muttered. "Matches... check. Flashlight...check. Cookies...check."

He had expected some commentary on this packing list from Wendell, but when he looked up, Wendell was staring out the window with an oddly distant expression.

"Wendell?"

"The moon," said Wendell dreamily. "The moon is...full."

Dreamy is not a normal state for iguanas. Danny stared at his friend in concern.

Were Wendell's teeth longer? Was the hair spreading? He always had bad posture, but was that a slouch or a hunch?

"I can almost hear it..."

Danny looked wildly around the room for something to snap Wendell out of his dreamy state. Unfortunately, Wendell was a compulsive neatnik, and the room was unnaturally clean. (In Danny's room, there would have been a dozen items in easy reach, suitable for braining lycanthropic best friends—softball bats, Ping-Pong paddles, plastic swords, rubber chickens. The only problem would be picking just one.)

He briefly considered grabbing the goldfish bowl and dumping the contents over Wendell's head, but Wendell would never forgive him if anything happened to Mister Fins. He'd had the goldfish since he was five.

"So...beautiful..." breathed Wendell.

Danny yanked a book off the bookcase—one of the comic collections of *Empire of Feathers,* softcover

but with definite heft—and smacked Wendell
across the back of the head with it.

"Right," said Danny briskly, "we've got to take out that alpha were-wurst. We clearly don't have much time."

"I'm allowed to think things are pretty!" snapped Wendell. "It doesn't mean anything!"

Danny gave him a look.

" . . . I'll get my flashlight," muttered Wendell.

Wendell's bedroom window did not have a convenient climbing tree, the way Danny's did, but it did overlook the attached garage. You just had to step out the window and you could walk around on the roof. From there, it was a short trip down to the rain gutter, which was nailed to the side of the house by slats that were almost as good as a ladder.

Danny went first, dropping into Wendell's mother's azaleas, and then waited impatiently while Wendell came down, one step at a time, his eyes squeezed tight.

They hurried around the side of the house and into the front yard. Danny scurried from shadow to shadow, hiding behind shrubs and hedges. Wendell plodded down the sidewalk in plain sight.

"There's nobody watching," said the iguana as Danny dove behind a garbage can.

"There might be ninjas!"

"We haven't seen ninjas around here for months."

They reached the storm drain at the end of the street without being attacked by ninjas, or spotted by grown-ups, and peered down into it. Danny turned on his flashlight and played the beam across the opening.

"Well," he said. "Here we are."

A car turned down at the end of the street, and both iguana and dragon ducked quickly behind a juniper hedge. The headlights washed across their hiding place, turning the black foliage briefly green, then the car crawled past. When the sound of the engine had faded, they slunk out onto the street.

"We'd better hurry," said Danny.

Wendell exhaled. He wanted to say, *Are you sure?* Or maybe *Do we have to?*

But it was Danny, and Danny was always sure, even when he was completely wrong. Wendell scratched at his back. The hair was definitely spreading. A few tufts between scales had grown into a patch as big as his palm. And the moon— he almost looked up at it, then hastily jerked his eyes back to the curb. Looking at the moon was bad. Looking at the moon made the whole world go kind of shivery and silver. His teeth felt strangely cold in his mouth, and when he ran his tongue delicately over them, they seemed larger than they had been.

"Hold my backpack," said Danny, and slid,

belly down and feetfirst, into the dark mouth of the drains.

He vanished. Wendell cringed.

A second later, Danny called up. "It's fine. Throw me the packs."

This is it, Wendell thought, tossing the bags and putting his glasses in his shirt pocket. The hole became a dark blur. It didn't really help.

"Come on!" hissed Danny.

There was open air under his feet and his tail, and the crumbling concrete lip of the drain scraped the back of his head. He dangled from his claw-tips for a second, unsure how far he was going to fall. Maybe he'd fall forever. Maybe the drains opened into a bottomless shaft, and the sewers poured into it, and he'd fall so far down that the earth's heart would open up beneath him—

"It's like six inches," said Danny, right beside him.

Wendell sighed and let go.

DOWN, DOWN, DOWN

The storm drain had a wide metal grate instead of a proper floor, and it was slick with dead leaves, old plastic bags, used gum wrappers, and other things that Danny didn't care to identify. The dragon swung the light briefly over the gunk-covered grate, and then to either side of it. A low corridor, made of a giant circular pipe, vanished into darkness.

"Which way do we go?" whispered Wendell.

"I'm not sure."

Danny turned the light to the wall, and found writing.

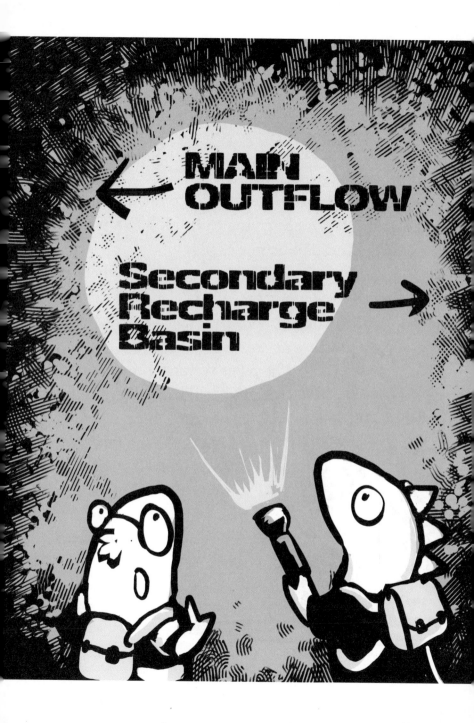

"Who do you think labeled these?" he asked.

"Sewage workers, I guess," said Wendell. He pushed his glasses up on his snout. "Main outflow gets us closer to the main sewer, I think. Where do you suppose the potato salad went?"

Danny frowned, trying to think like a potato salad. This did not come easily.

"I think it'd probably want to be where it could pick up more gunk," he said finally. "Kind of…grow a little. Let's try the main outflow."

The pipes weren't wide enough for two, so they walked single file, with Danny in front. Lots of gaps appeared overhead. They passed under a manhole cover, a little round cement room with metal ladder rungs bolted into the wall. The room was covered in graffiti, most of it words that would have shocked Wendell's mother.

HOW CAN YOU MISSPELL THAT? IT'S ONLY GOT FOUR LETTERS!

They had been walking for about ten minutes when the floor dropped into a series of steep concrete steps, each one with a deep rim. A thick layer of unidentifiable goop had formed in the resulting catch pools and squelched under their feet.

"Ugghhh . . ."

"I've seen worse," said Danny, hopping down to the next pool with a sound that was more slurp than splash.

WHEN HAVE YOU *POSSIBLY* SEEN WORSE?

REMEMBER LIVER SURPRISE DAY AT LUNCH?

The pipe opened up into a much larger chamber. The bottom of the room had a kind of walkway to one side, running along a deep, foamy canal of murky water. Pipes oozed wastewater. The air was warm and humid, like the indoor pool at the YRCA.*

The smell was incredible.

Danny and Wendell stopped in unspoken agree-

*The Young Reptiles' Christian Association, where Danny had spent many summers learning to swim and being yelled at for running next to the pool.

ment to try to get used to the stink. It was like old gym socks and hot garbage. Going into a stall in the boys' bathroom after Big Eddy had used it was like swimming in lilacs and fresh-baked bread by comparison.

Eventually they gave up. It wasn't so much getting used to it as just surrendering to it. Once Danny's eyes stopped watering and Wendell had finished cleaning his glasses every few seconds, they climbed the rest of the way down the staircase and onto the concrete walk.

"It's just like the sewer level in Dark Summons!" said Danny enthusiastically. "I played that like forty times!"

"Did you ever beat it?" asked Wendell.

"No. The last boss fight is like impossible. He throws flaming goats at you. I mean, c'mon! Flaming goats? That's just brutal."

Wendell knew that it was irrational, but he would have felt better if Danny had actually won the game, flaming goats notwithstanding.

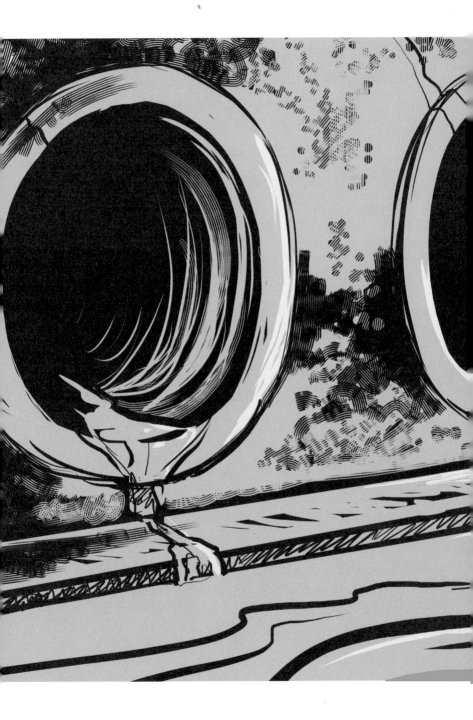

"I guess this is the main outflow," said the iguana, changing the subject. "But where do we go now?"

"Let's follow the walkway," said Danny. He may not have beaten the game, but he did know that paths usually went somewhere.

They followed the walkway. Stuff roiled in the water next to them, some of it recognizable, most of it not.

A hundred feet down, the walkway turned a corner, where a second massive chamber crossed the first. Danny and Wendell stopped at the corner, gazing helplessly across the massive outflow.

Since the notion of swimming did not appeal to anyone, they followed the walkway around the corner.

"I think I see a light up ahead," said Danny.

"A light? Down here?" Wendell wrung his tail in his hands. "I don't like it. What would make a light down here?"

"I don't know, but there is one." Danny switched off his flashlight, plunging them into sudden blackness. Wendell let out a little shriek, sending echoes scurrying through the tunnels like frightened mice.

But after a few seconds, Wendell did see something—a watery, wavery light, far off in the distance. "I guess—sort of—how could you tell?"

"Dragons have excellent eyesight."

They kept walking. The light got brighter, and then the walkway dead-ended in a iron-railed landing at an intersection of pipes. The light shone down through a hole overhead, casting a shifting circle on the water.

It was the moon. A *full* moon.

A shiver suddenly racked Danny, all his scales rubbing together.

This was it. This was the dream he'd had. The things he'd thought were trees weren't trees at all—they were the dark marks of water dripping down the walls, spreading out to form patterns like branches and tree roots. The moon was there, overhead, and reflected like a blob of mercury on the shifting, scummy water.

And Wendell—

"Do you hear it?" asked the iguana behind him, in a voice that didn't sound like Wendell at all.

"Hear what?" asked Danny, turning around with a sense of dread.

"The moon..." whispered the iguana. "I can hear it...singing..."

Behind his thick glasses, Wendell's eyes were glowing red.

"Wendell?"

A noise came from his friend that does not come from the throat of any reptile. It took Danny a moment to realize that Wendell was growling.

Danny considered. His friend was turning into one of the were-wurst's minions. If they were in a horror movie or a video game, this would be the moment where Danny was forced to slay his friend to save himself, or become a minion as well.

On the other hand, it was Wendell.

The iguana took a step forward, growling.

"Wendell!"

Wendell opened his mouth, revealing a wall of sharp teeth. He normally had eighty of them, but they weren't usually an inch long. The inside of his mouth looked like an ivory bear trap.

Danny weighed the options, leaned down, and splashed a handful of sewer water directly into Wendell's face.

"I . . . oh . . . jeez . . ." Wendell twisted his tail in his hands. "Sorry."

Danny sighed. The red was gone from Wendell's eyes, and that was the important thing. "It's fine. Just try not to do it again. Let's get you cured."

YOUR POTATOSHIP

Unfortunately, this was easier said than done. The walkway had ended, and the only option was to backtrack. And then ... possibly ... to swim.

Danny was really hoping it wouldn't come to that. Getting Wendell into the water would be nearly impossible, and he wasn't too keen on the idea himself. The water smelled so bad that even calling it "water" was optimistic.

—IT'S A RAT.

It was indeed a rat. It was large and sleek and longer than Danny's arm. It studied the pair thoughtfully, not as if they were menacing, but as if they were interesting birds that had wandered onto the rat's lawn.

"Maybe it can help us," said Danny.

Wendell looked at him as if his eyes were glowing red. "It's a rat."

"Rats are very intelligent," said Danny. He waved to the rat.

The rat did not wave back, but it did sit up on its hind legs expectantly.

128

"We're looking for an old friend of ours. A, uh, potato salad." Danny mimed a big, vaguely lumpy shape. "We think it lives down here."

The rat appeared to consider this.

"Are you expecting an answer?" asked Wendell.

"Don't be stupid," said Danny, "rats can't talk."

The rat turned and scurried into the dark pipe.

NOW WHO'S STUPID?

"Just wait . . . " said Danny, waving a hand at him.

The rat reappeared, made an impatient squeak, and ran back into the pipe. Its expression said clearly: Are you guys coming, or what?

Following the rat was a little tricky. Danny had to swing himself over the balcony and step down into the pipe, and then grab for Wendell when he did the same. Once inside the pipe, they had to walk bent over.

"At least we're not swimming," said Wendell.

The rat scurried ahead of them, stopping frequently to peer back at them and chitter.

"Do you think it's really leading us to the potato salad?" asked Wendell worriedly.

"Absolutely," said Danny. "This sort of thing

happens all the time. It's totally mythological. Heroes follow the animal guide and it leads them to awesome adventures!"

"Seriously?"

"It happened to my cousin. He followed a white peacock for three days."

"Where'd he wind up?"

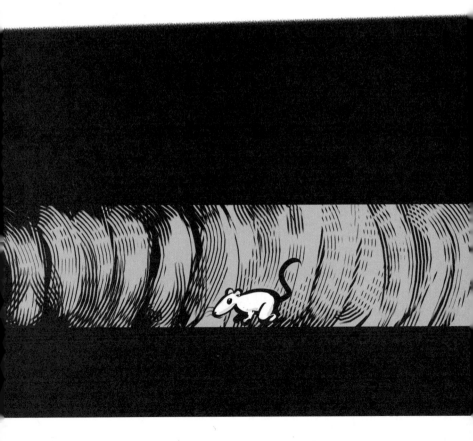

"The mall," Danny admitted. "But he got a great deal on a plasma-screen TV, so it totally worked out."

"Joseph Campbell is spinning in his grave," muttered Wendell.

"Who?"

"Never mind."

The pipe crossed another, larger pipe, and the rat turned left down it. They followed.

A few minutes later, they reached a larger room. The rat hopped nimbly from the mouth of the pipe to a nearby walkway, and Danny and Wendell followed, scrambling over the railing.

The walkway ran around the edge of the circular room, which fell away into darkness below.

The rat hurried around the walkway, to a narrow doorway. In it sat another rat.

The first rat pointed a paw back at Danny and Wendell and squeaked.

It's always awkward to have people talk about you as if you're not there. It's significantly more awkward when it's being done by a pair of small rodents. Danny and Wendell stood and fidgeted.

The second rat stepped aside. The first rat—the one that Danny was thinking of as their rat—chittered cheerfully and hurried through the doorway.

"What's happening?" muttered Wendell.

"I don't know. I don't speak Rodent," said Danny. "But I think the one is a guard, and our rat just told him we were cool."

They followed their guide through the door. As they passed the guard-rat, Danny bobbed his head politely to it. It met his eyes with its small, beady black ones, let out a rat-sized sigh, and looked away.

Their rat led them into a maze of tunnels, turning left and right so rapidly that Danny was hard-pressed to keep the rat in the bobbing circle of the flashlight.

"I'm completely lost," moaned Wendell.

"So am I," Danny admitted. "But I'm sure the rat will lead us back afterward."

"What if he doesn't?"

"It'll be fine, Wendell."

Danny was glad to hear that turning into a were-wiener hadn't affected his best friend's ability to sigh very, very loudly.

The last tunnel was much lower than the

others. Danny and Wendell had to drop to their knees and crawl through it.

"Slow down!" begged Wendell.

The rat looked back and squeaked at them, but waited.

The low pipe only lasted for a few turns, which was good, as far as Danny was concerned. Wendell was pressed so close behind him that he kept kneeling on the dragon's tail.

"Wendell! Tail!"

"Sorry," said Wendell, "but it's dark back here!"

"There's a light up ahead," said Danny.

The rat stopped in the mouth of the pipe. Danny came up behind it and looked out over its head.

"Oh..."

"What is it?" Wendell demanded. "What?"

The potato salad's lair was a large circular room, crammed with trash and refuse. There were broken chairs, old egg cartons, junked roller skates, discarded brooms. There were dustpans, dustbins, dust bunnies, and broken DustBusters. Danny couldn't see the walls for the piles of trash.

On every surface perched rats—big ones, little ones, black and white, scurrying and still. Most of them were watching the newcomers.

Their rat hopped down and gestured to them with a paw. Danny gulped and stepped out of the pipe, his feet making wet noises on the soggy cardboard that covered the floor.

"What? Why—oh..."

At the end of the room, enthroned on more junk, squatted the vast form of the potato salad.

"It's huge ..." breathed Wendell. "How did it get so big?"

"Well..." Danny stared at it. His old lunch was now ten times as big as Danny himself. "Whenever she peels potatoes, Mom dumps the skins into the garbage disposal in the sink. If that happens every time, and all the potato bits came down here..."

As if to confirm this hypothesis, a rat ran in from the side of the room, carrying a small bit of something white in one paw. It trotted up to the swollen potato salad, and patted the little white bit—a chunk of raw potato?—into the side of the salad, then ran off with a satisfied squeak.

"The rats are feeding it," said Danny. "Or... err... growing it, anyway."

"That is either amazingly cool or incredibly gross," said Wendell.

"No reason it can't be both."

Their rat marched down the aisle of trash as well as a rat can march. It halted several feet from the potato salad's throne, went up on its hind legs, and bowed. Then it squeaked, pointed back at Wendell and Danny, and squeaked again.

Danny and Wendell followed the rat, stopping well back from the throne. Wendell said, "Errr." Danny waved.

A glopping, glorbling noise came from the salad, a sort of sticky rumbling belch. The vast mound of potato bits leaned forward. Dozens of beady black eyes watched from around the room.

HI! REMEMBER US?

There was a long awful moment when Danny thought he'd miscalculated the gratitude of a renegade school lunch.

What if the potato salad didn't remember? Would the rats attack? Could he breathe fire to keep them off if they did? Would the Tabasco sauce even work on rats?

Then the potato salad belched a long positive note. The rat squeaked happily. All over the room, the rats relaxed.

SEE? I TOLD YOU IT'D REMEMBER US!

"So anyway," Danny said, "it's great to see you! You've got a great place down here!"

Wendell started to mutter something about the smell, and Danny kicked him in the ankle. The potato salad gave another enthusiastic belch.

"Anyway, we came down here to ask for your help."

The potato salad growled wetly. Wendell cringed. "I know!" Danny said. "They're totally awful! And of course, everybody knows that potato salad and hot dogs are ancient enemies—"

Rats nodded around the room. Wendell rolled his eyes. "Am I the only person on earth that doesn't know this?"

"—so of course we thought of you."

The potato salad gurgled thoughtfully. Danny grew slightly more hopeful.

"The alpha wurst is holed up somewhere near the cafeteria," he explained. "And we think we can take it out—we have silver skewers and everything—but the problem is the minions. Almost all the kids at school are infected, and will try to protect their leader. So we were hoping you could—y'know—go up there and hold them off."

A dubious gurgle. The potato salad shuffled in its throne.

The potato salad didn't seem to be buying it. Danny wondered if he'd overestimated the hatred between wieners and potato salad.

Wendell stepped forward. "Um—Your Potato-ship?"

The potato salad didn't exactly have eyes, but there was a definite shift of attention to Wendell.

"One of the minions we're worried about is Big Eddy. The one who tried to eat you. You bit his hand. Do you remember him?"

Wet, volcanic laughter filled the room.

Apparently the salad DID remember Big Eddy.

"So if you or the rats could help us stop Big Eddy and the others, we'd be really grateful."

"Good thinking!" whispered Danny.

Wendell scuffed at the ground with one foot.

The potato salad considered for a moment, and then it . . . well, it couldn't really stand up, but it seemed to ooze into a more upright position. Long gloppy growths, like arms, extended, and the potato salad lifted them overhead.

Whatever it was doing, the rats seemed hypnotized. They swayed in time to the belching noises. Danny and Wendell stood and listened politely, even though neither one could tell what was being said.

"Maybe he's saying 'Let's crush the minions!'" Danny whispered.

"Maybe he's saying 'Let's eat the dragon and use the iguana's bones for toothpicks,'" muttered Wendell.

The potato salad roared. A squeaky cheer went up from the assembled rats.

The salad let its arms drop and turned its attention back to Danny and Wendell.

"You'll help, then?" asked Danny.

An affirmative rumble. Rats nodded and their guide rat chased its own tail in delight.

"Great! Thank you! Uh—tomorrow at lunchtime, then? That's when we'll make our move, if you want to ... uh ... send troops ... "

The potato salad twisted in an approximation

of a nod, then settled back into its throne. The rats began leaving the room, streams of furry bodies funneling into pipes and down drains.

Their guide rat sat up, tugged at Danny's shirt, then led them toward the drain. Apparently their visit was at an end.

WELL— UH—THANKS! GOOD TO SEE YOU!

GLORP!

"I think that went well," said Danny as the rat led them back through the tunnels.

"We'll find out tomorrow," said Wendell.

FOOD FIGHT!

Danny had thought that yesterday afternoon was long, but this morning was way worse. He couldn't concentrate. Would the rats come to help? Would they be able to communicate?

In the desk next to him, Wendell itched. He looked terrible. If he was being honest, Danny would say that he didn't look so great himself. They hadn't gotten back from the sewers until three in the morning.

A number of students were missing. Apparently the itching had alerted their parents that something was wrong. As far as Danny was concerned, that was fine—it meant fewer minions.

Big Eddy, unfortunately, was not one of the ones who had stayed home. He didn't look well at all.

"Now, students . . ." said Mr. Snaug, "take out your social studies textbook."

Danny winced. He'd left his books at home, in order to fit the silverware in his backpack.

"Mr. Dragonbreath?" asked Mr. Snaug wearily. "Your textbook?"

"I—uh—forgot it, Mr. Snaug."

"Share with Wendell, then." His teacher sighed.

"Cheer up," whispered Danny. "Just another hour until lunch!"

Wendell looked sick. He felt like he was waiting for the dentist. What if they couldn't find the alpha wurst? What if the skewer didn't work?

What if Big Eddy threw them through a wall?

Plus, he itched. It was even worse than the one time he got a mosquito bite on his eyelid. He itched in places he hadn't known could itch, between his toes and under his tongue and behind his eyes. His brain itched.

When the lunch bell rang, Wendell was so sunk in misery that he didn't comprehend what it was.

"C'mon!" said Danny. "It's time!"

Wendell dragged himself to his feet like an iguana going to his execution.

Danny's pack clinked as they walked.

They got through the lunch line and stood with trays in their hands, stumped. "Err...what do we do now?" asked Wendell.

"I was sort of hoping the rats would be here," muttered Danny.

"Well, they aren't." Wendell frowned. "We need to get into the kitchen. The wurst has to be back there somewhere."

"Are you sure?"

Wendell scratched at his neck. "I think so. It sort of...itches more in that direction."

He had not previously realized that you could itch directionally. Wendell could have gone on quite happily without knowing that.

"The lunch ladies aren't gonna just let us back there," said Danny. "Some of them might be minions too..."

That there might be grown-up minions had not occurred to Wendell. He groaned.

WE'RE DOOMED.

WE'RE NOT DOOMED! WE JUST NEED A DISTRACTION!

Big Eddy crossed the cafeteria, two tables away. Danny grinned suddenly. "I think I know just the thing."

He picked up his slice of pizza. Orange grease dripped off the cheese. He took aim.

He fired.

"Bull's-eye!" Danny crowed.

Big Eddy roared, pizza dripping off his head, then whipped around, searching for his unknown assailant. Unable to spot one immediately, he threw his own slice of pizza wildly into the crowd.

Wendell, seeing Danny's plan in action, grabbed his own open milk carton and flung it. His aim was terrible, and instead of Big Eddy, he hit a third-grade newt on top of the head. She began shrieking and throwing handfuls of french fries.

The kids of Herpitax-Phibbias School for Reptiles and Amphibians temporarily forgot their mysterious itching, their unexplained hair, and the presence of authority figures. As one, they rose, responding to that most ancient of battle cries.

"FOOD FIGHT!"

Danny was having so much fun flinging food that he almost forgot they had a mission. Then Wendell grabbed him and yanked him to one side.

The lunch ladies poured from the back of the cafeteria, ready to do battle. In the general confusion, Wendell and Danny slipped behind them and into the kitchen. "Where to?" whispered Danny.

"I . . . uh . . . left, I think, but . . . oh, it itches!" Wendell had to stop in the middle of the room and scratch furiously. His scales were starting to come off. Danny winced in sympathy.

They peered down the hallway toward the freezers. At least, Danny peered. Wendell just huddled and scratched.

"This way?" asked Danny. Wendell grunted, sounding not unlike the potato salad. They hurried down the hallway, still hearing cries and splatters of food from the main cafeteria.

Danny paused outside the walk-in freezer where he'd found the were-wiener package, but Wendell didn't. He was holding his head and blinking his eyes a lot, but he stumbled forward. Danny followed, wondering where the iguana was headed.

"Down here," panted Wendell. "It's got to be close . . ."

Danny remembered the lunch lady saying something about the Big Freezer. Could it be the home of the alpha were-wurst?

Apparently so. Wendell had halted. "In here," he said, eyes scrunched closed. "It's got to be in here. Oh God, it itches!"

Danny dropped his back-pack and rummaged inside. He came up with the big-gest fork, a meat server with glittering tines.

The Big Freezer was even colder than the smaller one. Ice crystals slicked the walls. Their breath hung in the air like fog.

Wendell felt strangely better. The cold seemed

to help the itch. He didn't want to scratch his own eyes out anymore. Unfortunately there was something else—a kind of hissing in his brain, something that slithered over and under the edges of actual sound, so he wasn't sure if he was hearing it or just thinking it.

It was a little like he'd felt looking at the moon.

Danny didn't know what he'd expected—sides of beef hanging from the ceiling, maybe—but it was just giant racks, holding boxes and mysterious tubs as big as his torso. "BUTTER" said one in big letters, and "VEGETABLE OIL." "LARD" said another.

"Eww . . ." said Wendell. "That can't be healthy."

"You can write a letter to the principal after we're out of here." Danny brandished his fork. "We've got wurst to slay."

"Can't ... let you ... do that ... dorkbreath ..."
hissed a deep voice behind them.

With infinite dread, Danny turned.

In the doorway, he saw a massive, slump-shouldered silhouette. Big Eddy.

His eyes were glowing red.

BARBEQUE

"We're dead," said Wendell.

Danny didn't answer him. Behind Big Eddy, there were more kids, and worse yet, two of the lunch ladies. All of them had glowing red eyes.

The lunch ladies were almost worse than Big Eddy. Danny hated Big Eddy, he was terrified of him, but the Komodo dragon was only a kid. (A mountain-sized kid, but still.) The lunch ladies were grown-ups. You didn't fight grown-ups.

Whether it was the fear or the excitement, he didn't know, but the back of Danny's throat was burning. His chest felt hot and tight, and smoke was leaking out of his nostrils and mixing with the fog of breath in the freezer. He felt dangerous.

STAND BACK!

Nobody stood back. Big Eddy actually took a couple of steps forward. Apparently Danny didn't sound as dangerous as he felt.

Wendell gulped. Danny would have, but his

throat was burning so bad that he thought he might throw up if he did.

"I'm gonna break you in half, dorkbreath," rumbled Big Eddy.

Danny retreated a half step. He would have gone farther, but he'd run into one of the shelves. The metal was cold against his back, and the tubs of lard and margarine rubbed against his scales.

Big Eddy cleared the doorway. One of the lunch ladies pressed in behind him, holding a ladle aloft. It was Ms. Woggenthal. Her eyes were the color of tomato sauce and glowed in the dim light of the freezer.

Somewhere off to Danny's left, Wendell moaned.

Just then there was a skritching noise from the shelf above him. Danny tore his gaze away from the bully and looked up.

A large gray rat looked down at him and fired off a tiny salute. He couldn't be sure, but he thought it might be the same one that had led them through the tunnels.

Danny exhaled in sudden relief. Smoke poured out of his mouth. The rat looked surprised.

The Komodo dragon's brow knitted in confusion. "Are you—"

Whatever he was about to say was drowned out in a sudden wave of squeaking.

The rats had finally arrived.

Furry gray bodies flowed down the hallway, swarming up the legs of the were-minions. Kids shrieked and slapped at the rats.

"Rats!?" yelled Ms. Woggenthal. "In my kitchen?!" She spun around. Her eyes were still rather red, but Danny suspected it had more to do with rage than the were-wurst. She waded through the horde of rats, using the ladle like a club.

"They're everywhere!" someone screamed from down the hall. "Oh my God, they're in the soup!"

Big Eddy frowned. He was not a particularly quick thinker, and things were coming at him entirely too fast. There were rats climbing up his arm and legs. He frowned down at them and slowly lifted a hand the size of a dinner plate.

The rat perched above Danny's head launched itself through the air.

"Rat! Be careful!" cried Wendell. "Duck, Danny!"

The rat leaped over Danny to Big Eddy's head. Big Eddy roared and slapped at the top of his skull, but the rat was too fast. It scurried around the Komodo dragon's head, grabbing on to the tufts of hair that had sprouted from his scalp.

The last Danny and Wendell saw of Big Eddy, he was lumbering out of the freezer, flailing his arms and trying to escape. The rat was using his hair like reins. Big Eddy's yells and the rat's delighted squeaks faded into the distance.

Danny peered around the door frame. There was no one in the hallway, but Danny caught a brief glimpse of a shadow across the wall—the silhouette of a very large rat, and atop it, a lumpy irregular form, riding into battle.

The potato salad had come through. Danny and Wendell were alone in the freezer with the alpha wurst.

FOLLOW THE TRAIL

"Okay," said Danny. "Okay." He exhaled a cloud of smoke. Wendell coughed.

There was a rustling in the back of the freezer. The boys whipped around.

"Was that it? Was that the alpha?"

"You tell me," Danny said.

Wendell scratched helplessly at his neck and shrugged.

Danny picked up his skewering fork and began creeping toward the back of the freezer. Wendell followed.

Everything looked normal and orderly. The lunch ladies ran a tight ship. Nothing screamed of the presence of a diabolical hot dog from Transylvania.

"There!" said Wendell. "On the floor!"

Red splotches had frozen to the freezer floor. Danny crouched and poked one.

"Oh noooo, it's blood," whimpered Wendell.

> NO, IT'S KETCHUP. WE'RE CLOSE.

The trail of red led down the aisle and into the dark back corner of the freezer. It was easy to follow. The wurst hadn't bothered to hide.

They peered around the edge of the shelves.

"Is it in there?" asked Wendell.

"I don't know..." Danny crept closer. He reached out with the silver fork and lifted the edge of a piece of trash. "It must be in here somewh—"

A growl arose from inside the nest, a deep, bone-rattling sound. Wendell gulped.

Danny took a step back.

The pile of boxes and tub lids began to thrash, and then, slowly, a red back breached the surface.

The alpha wurst reared and looked at them.

Danny hadn't expected it to be so big. He'd been thinking it was the size of a hot dog, maybe one of the big kielbasas from the grocery story, not a giant sausage bigger than he was.

It had teeth too. Big ones. Drool mixed with ketchup dripped from its jaws.

Danny held up his silver fork. It looked very small in his hands.

Still, it was silver.

The wurst hissed.

"Wendell," said Danny, not taking his eyes off the meat-beast, "open my backpack and get more silverware. You'll have to distract it so that I can skewer it."

The wurst made a strange globbering noise. It took Danny a moment to realize that it was laughing.

"Wendell?"

I'M AFRAID I CAN'T DO THAT, DANNY.

"This is not a good time to lose your mind, Wendell!" Danny circled the wurst, moving away from his friend. It had been easy to snap the iguana out of it before, but with the alpha wurst right there . . .

"It's in my head," said Wendell dreamily. "It's telling me to stop you . . . "

"Don't listen!" Danny tried to move in closer to the wurst, but Wendell was in the way.

Danny was pretty sure that he could take Wendell in a fight, but the iguana was his best friend, and he didn't want to hurt him. Also, there was a good chance Danny'd get bitten, and who knew what would happen then?

Wendell took a clumsy swing at him. Danny leaned back to avoid it.

WENDELL, I DON'T WANT TO HAVE TO BREATHE FIRE AT YOU!

OH COME ON, DANNY. YOU *KNOW* YOU CAN'T BREATHE FIRE.

It occurred to Danny that pummeling Wendell might not be that bad after all.

No, no. Best friend. Possessed by wurst. Doesn't mean what he says.

"What would your mother think?" the dragon tried. "You know you can't get into a good college if you're controlled by a giant hot dog."

Bizarrely, this actually seemed to stop Wendell. The iguana halted in his tracks, frowning. Danny inched sideways, closer to the wurst, which was swaying overhead like a giant cobra.

His chest ached. His throat burned. Smoke was leaking out his nostrils and making his eyes water.

Think hot thoughts, his dad was always saying. *Focus your chi. Invoke the energy of fire,* his great-grandfather had told him, during the bit with the ninjas.

He could do this. He could breathe fire. Probably.

If he could just get close enough . . .

"It's saying it can get me a scholarship," said Wendell slowly.

"Oh come ON," said Danny, and hauled off and smacked Wendell's glasses off his face.

MY GLASSES!

It was all the opening Danny needed. He spun toward the startled alpha wurst, took a breath so deep that his ribs nearly cracked, and breathed fire.

The dying wurst bucked wildly, sending Danny rolling to the freezer floor. There was smoke everywhere. It smelled like the world's biggest wienie roast. The wurst keened, the fork still sticking out of its skin, then began to shrink. The overstretched sausage casing deflated like a balloon. Soon there was nothing left but a puddle of smoking ketchup and the gleaming silver fork.

Wendell found his glasses and put them back on his nose. There was a crack in one lens, but his eyes were no longer red. "Is that—did it—?"

"I think it's roasted," said Danny, standing up and feeling for bruises. He was going to be black and blue tomorrow. "How are you?"

Wendell frowned. "I don't itch anymore. And"—he ran his hands over his scales—"look!"

NO HAIR!

"It worked." Danny sighed with relief, adding more smoke to the already smoggy freezer.

"I breathed fire," he said to Wendell.

"You did," said Wendell.

"We should probably get out of here." He picked up the fork and stashed it in his pack.

"Yeah."

"I'm starving all of a sudden."

"Me too."

"I don't think I want hot dogs."

"Definitely not," said Wendell.

"Smells good, though," said Danny.

"Oh, yeah."

Arms draped over each other's shoulders, they limped toward the freezer door.

SUSPENSION

Danny couldn't have been happier. Even the two solid weeks of detention he'd gotten for starting a food fight couldn't dampen his spirits. The alpha wurst was dead, Wendell was hairless again, and all the other kids had recovered from their bites.

Best of all, the school had closed for five whole days while the health inspector tried to get to the bottom of the rat invasion. Life just did not get better than that.

They relaxed in Wendell's room. Mister Fins swam cheerful circles in his bowl. It was a perfect day.

"I hope Ms. Woggenthal doesn't get in trouble," said Wendell gloomily. "She was pretty nice."

Danny rolled his eyes. In the middle of a spectacularly sunny day, you could always rely on Wendell to find a cloud. Usually with cloud-rabies or something.

SHE'S FINE, WENDELL. MOM SAID THAT THEY THINK THE RATS GOT PUSHED UP FROM THE SEWER BECAUSE OF ALL THE RAIN, AND THEY DIDN'T FIND ANY TRACE OF THE POTATO SALAD AT ALL.

WELL, THEY'D NEVER BELIEVE THE *REAL* STORY...

"Any more luck breathing fire?"

Danny shrugged. "Sort of. It seems to help if it's really cold. I tried sticking my head in the freezer this morning, and I melted a bag of frozen peas."

"You think Big Eddy will stop stealing your lunch now?"

"I dunno." Danny propped his snout on his hand. "All the minions seem to have forgotten what happened."

"I remember," said Wendell, shuddering. "I'm really sorry that I tried to—"

Danny waved a hand. "Yeah, but you didn't do anything, really. It's fine."

Wendell tapped moodily on Mister Fins's bowl.

"So what do you want to do today?" asked Danny, making an effort to change the subject.

Wendell groaned. "I dunno. Mom's worried that I'm going to forget my education while school's closed, and I'll never catch up, and won't get into a good college and be doomed to a life of destitution on the streets."

"No . . ."

"There's pigeons and fish and stuff! And somebody spray-painted this huge mural on the bottom of the bridge, so you can only see if you stand under it. It's really neat!"

"In Birchbark Park? Really?" Wendell pushed his glasses up on his snout.

"Plus there's a storm drain there. We might even see our buddy the rat!"

"What are we waiting for?" asked Wendell.

His mother's voice drifted up. "Wendell, honey? Don't forget to review your periodic table . . ."

Danny and Wendell exchanged glances.

It was a spectacular day. Sure, two weeks of detention would be bad, but not until the school reopened, and that was five days away. Anything could happen in five days.

Anything at all.